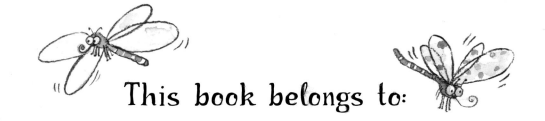

This book belongs to:

_____

For my husband Phil and our precious Tinysauruses: Sean, Bethany, Joey and Katy. Love. S.W.

For Poppy, with love. J.F.

First published in Great Britain in 2010 by Andersen Press Ltd.,

20 Vauxhall Bridge Road, London SW1V 2SA.

Published in Australia by Random House Australia Pty.,

Level 3, 100 Pacific Highway, North Sydney, NSW 2060.

Text copyright © Sheryl Webster, 2010. Illustration copyright © Jan Fearnley, 2010.

The rights of Sheryl Webster and Jan Fearnley to be identified as the author

and illustrator of this work have been asserted by them in accordance with the

Copyright, Designs and Patents Act, 1988. All rights reserved.

Colour separated in Switzerland by Photolitho AG, Zurich.

Printed and bound in Singapore by Tien Wah Press.

Jan Fearnley has used graphite pencil and watercolour in this book.

10   9   8   7   6   5   4   3   2   1

British Library Cataloguing in Publication Data available.

ISBN 978 1 84939 010 1 (Hardback)

ISBN 978 1 84939 029 3 (Paperback)

This book has been printed on acid-free paper

TINYSAURUS

Sheryl Webster   Jan Fearnley

Andersen Press

Tinysaurus was tiny. He had tiny teeth, tiny claws, and a teeny tiny roar. But Tinysaurus wanted to be big like Daddysaurus.

Daddysaurus had **huge** teeth, gigantic claws, and an **enormous**

roooooooar!

Tinysaurus would even settle for just being as big as his elder sister,

BIGsissysaurus.

It wasn't as if he hadn't tried to get bigger. He had.

He had tried jumping
up and **down**
. . . but that didn't work.

He had tried
streeeeeeeeetching
himself on a tree branch . . .
but he couldn't hold
on for long enough.

He had tried tying tree
trunks to his legs . . .

. . . but the only thing that
was made bigger were the
bumps on his head.

It just
wasn't fair!

Being tiny meant that Mummysaurus would not let him go to the Plippy Ploppy Waterhole on his own. Bigsissysaurus could.

Nor could he go to the Sludgy Squelchy Swamp. Bigsissysaurus could.

He wasn't even allowed to graze on his own in the Swishy Swashy Grassland. Bigsissysaurus could.

And he was absolutely forbidden to go near the Ooh~Ouch Mountain. But even Bigsissysaurus was not allowed to go there!

But the one thing
Tinysaurus was
most sad
about . . .

. . . was
being too
tiny to look
after the eggs
for Mummysaurus
on his own.

Tinysaurus loved the eggs.
He sat and watched
the nest.

He nuzzled them.
He turned them.
He talked to them.

He could not wait
for them to hatch.

One day, while Mummysaurus and Daddysaurus were out hunting, a shadow fell over Tinysaurus and the ground shook.

He looked up to see a huge Nastysaurus eyeing up the eggs. "Mmmmm, supper," it snarled.

The Nastysaurus swiped at Bigsissysaurus
with his tail, knocking her flying.

"Got to save the eggs!" Tinysaurus thought.

The Nastysaurus tried to swipe at him, but
Tinysaurus was so tiny that he kept missing.

Tinysaurus balanced the nest carefully and ran.

"Run, Tinysaurus, run!"

Bigsissysaurus shouted.

Tinysaurus ran towards the Plippy Ploppy Waterhole.

PLIP . . . PLOP . . . PLIP . . . PLOP . . .

The water was so deep that it almost washed over him . . .
but he ran on.

He came to the Sludgy Squelchy
Swamp.

Sludge . . . Squelch . . .

Sludge . . . Squelch . . .

His tiny feet almost got stuck.

A quick dart out, and into the Swishy Swashy Grassland.

Swish . . . Swash . . .   Swish . . Swash . . .

Tinysaurus belted along but, oh no, he'd been spotted! The Nastysaurus was *so close*. Tinysaurus looked ahead and saw . . .

. . . the **Ooh~Ouch** Mountain.

He took a deep breath and . . . ran.
Ooh~Ouch . . . Ooh~Ouch . . . Ooh~Ouch . . . Ooh~Ouch.
His toes were singed, but still he kept going.
He just hoped the eggs didn't boil!

At the top, Tinysaurus spotted a small hole in the side of the mountain. He was just the right size to squeeze inside it.

The Nastysaurus

came closer . . .

. . . and closer

. . . and closer!

It poked in its snout. Its huge jaws snapped at Tinysaurus.

And then the Nastysaurus couldn't move in,
and it couldn't move out. It was stuck!

Tinysaurus quickly sneaked out underneath him.

The Nastysaurus was furious.

Mummysaurus and Daddysaurus came huffing and puffing up. "Are you okay?" they panted. Tinysaurus nodded.

"Are you angry with me for coming up here?" he asked.
They both nuzzled him closely.

"How could we be angry?
You've saved the eggs! You're a hero."

The next morning Tinysaurus had a lovely surprise.
There in the nest were three babysauruses.
They had tiny teeth, tiny claws and teeny tiny roars.
Tinysaurus grinned an enormous grin.

"You know what this means?" he said.
"I'm not a TINYSAURUS any more.

I'm a BIGbrosaurus!"

And he was the best Bigbrosaurus ever.

More great books to enjoy:

9781849390088

9781849390774

9781849390361

THE TALENT SHOW

Jo Hodgkinson

9781849390460

9781842709443